Praise for
*Mindy Kim and the
Yummy Seaweed Business*

★ "A lovingly authentic debut
that shines."

–*Kirkus Reviews*, starred review

Mindy Kim and the
Birthday Puppy

**Don't miss more fun adventures
with Mindy Kim!**

Mindy Kim

and the
Birthday Puppy

BOOK
3

By Lyla Lee
Illustrated by Dung Ho

ALADDIN
New York London Toronto Sydney New Delhi

This book is a work of fiction. Any references to historical events, real people, or real places are used fictitiously. Other names, characters, places, and events are products of the author's imagination, and any resemblance to actual events or places or persons, living or dead, is entirely coincidental.

🐦 ALADDIN
An imprint of Simon & Schuster Children's Publishing Division
1230 Avenue of the Americas, New York, New York 10020
First Aladdin paperback edition May 2020
Text copyright © 2020 by Lyla Lee
Illustrations copyright © 2020 by Dung Ho
Also available in an Aladdin hardcover edition.
All rights reserved, including the right of reproduction in whole or in part in any form.
ALADDIN and related logo are registered trademarks of Simon & Schuster, Inc.
For information about special discounts for bulk purchases, please contact Simon & Schuster Special Sales at 1-866-506-1949 or business@simonandschuster.com.
The Simon & Schuster Speakers Bureau can bring authors to your live event. For more information or to book an event contact the Simon & Schuster Speakers Bureau at 1-866-248-3049 or visit our website at www.simonspeakers.com.
Designed by Laura Lyn DiSiena
The illustrations for this book were rendered digitally.
The text of this book was set in Haboro.
Manufactured in the United States of America 0420 OFF
10 9 8 7 6 5 4 3 2 1
Library of Congress Control Number 2020932432
ISBN 978-1-5344-4014-2 (hc)
ISBN 978-1-5344-4013-5 (pbk)
ISBN 978-1-5344-4015-9 (eBook)

For Lulu the Goldendoodle
and all the other dogs in my life.
You're the best!

Mindy Kim and the
Birthday Puppy

Chapter 1

My name is Mindy Kim. I am eight years old.

That's right—not seven, not seven and a half, but EIGHT.

Today is my birthday!

"Yay!" I jumped out of my bed with Mr. Toe Beans, my corgi stuffed doll.

The sun was shining bright outside, and even from inside my room, I could tell it was a beautiful day! And the best part? It was a Friday, and I was going to have a party after school with all my friends. I was so excited!

"Happy birthday, Mindy!" my dad said as he

opened my bedroom door. "How does it feel to be eight?"

I quickly hid Mr. Toe Beans behind my back before Dad could see. I was eight now! I didn't want Dad to think I still slept with a stuffed animal. Big kids didn't sleep with dolls, and the bigger of a kid I seemed, the more likely it was that Dad would buy me a puppy. Dad had said he'd get me a puppy for my birthday. And today was finally the day!

"Good! I feel so big now!"

Dad put a hand to his chin, like he was thinking really hard as he looked at me. "Hmm, you do seem a bit taller than you did yesterday."

"Really?" I bit my lip with excitement.

Dad laughed. "I'm just messing with you. But don't worry, sweetie. You're definitely still growing! Come down and eat some seaweed soup! Let's call your grandparents!"

Every birthday, I eat seaweed soup for breakfast. It's a Korean tradition! And then we call my grandparents in Korea so they can wish me happy birthday before they go to sleep. Korea time is thirteen hours ahead of Florida, so it was already nine p.m. there.

Mom used to always make seaweed soup for me, but since she wasn't here this year, Dad made it. It wasn't as good as Mom's, but I didn't tell him that. I didn't want to hurt his feelings.

Dad brought his laptop to the dining room table as I ate. Grandma and Grandpa were already on the screen, their smiles wide and eyes shining. They looked so happy to see me! And I was happy to see them, too.

"Saeng-il chook-ha-hae, Min-jung-ah!" said Grandpa, wishing me happy birthday in Korean. He used my Korean name, like everyone else did back in Korea.

"Gomap seum-nida!" I said thanks, bowing with respect.

My grandparents asked me a lot of questions about how I was doing and what I was going to do today. They always ask me lots of stuff when we talk, because we only call each other on special days. I don't know how to call my grandparents in

Korea by myself, and Dad is usually too busy to do it for me on regular days.

When we were done catching up, Dad put away his laptop and joined me at the table with his bowl of seaweed soup. I was done eating by then, but I remained sitting to keep Dad company.

"Dad," I asked, "why do we eat seaweed soup on our birthdays?"

"It's because a lot of mothers in Korea eat sea-weed soup after they have their babies. Seaweed is full of nutrients that are really good for the moms."

Dad mentioning mothers reminded me of Mom and how she wasn't here to celebrate my birthday. And then I realized that she wasn't going to be here for any of my other birthdays, either. That made me really sad, all of a sudden.

"Are you excited for your party later today, Mindy?" Dad asked with a smile.

"Yes!" I said, trying to smile back.

Dad frowned, as if he knew what I was thinking. I'm a really bad liar.

"Your mom would be so proud of you, Mindy,"

he said. "It was hard, but you adjusted so well to living here. And you have so many friends now!"

"Thanks, Appa," I replied, feeling kind of grown-up.

I was looking forward to my party today, but I was also looking forward to getting a puppy for my birthday, just like my dad had said. But I didn't mention that part. I didn't want to ruin the surprise.

Chapter 2

At school, Mrs. Potts gave me a cute balloon that said IT'S MY BIRTHDAY TODAY! I also got to wear a gold paper crown on my head. I felt so special!

The class sang me "Happy Birthday," like we do for everyone's birthdays. I had a big smile the entire time they were singing. I felt so lucky and grateful!

"So, Mindy," Mrs. Potts said after they were done. "Before we get started with our class today, why don't you tell everyone what you plan on doing for your birthday?"

"I'm having a party!" I said. "And everyone in the class is invited!"

Several kids said "Yay!" and clapped with

excitement. Dad had already e-mailed the other parents about the party, so I knew not everyone could come, but I still wanted to say everyone was invited all the same.

"And," I added, "I think my dad is getting me a . . . puppy!"

The class gasped. Some kids even squealed!

"You *think*?" Mrs. Potts asked, looking confused.

"It's supposed to be a surprise, but I saw my dad looking at shelter websites on his tablet. And he said he would get me a puppy if I was grown-up and responsible enough!"

"Well, I'm wishing you the best today, Mindy," said Mrs. Potts. "I hope you have a wonderful day!"

Besides that morning, though, it was a pretty normal day of school. The only other thing that was different was that people who saw my golden crown in the hallway or in the cafeteria wished me happy birthday. When I first came to this school, I didn't think anyone would be nice to me, but now everyone was really friendly.

At recess, Sally let me have *two* turns on the swings. It made me so happy!

After I was done, I gave her a hug. "I'm so grateful you're my friend!"

Sally smiled. "I'm grateful you're my friend too!"

When school finally ended, I gathered up all my friends who were coming to my birthday party.

"I'll see everyone there! Be sure to come. We're going to have pizza, cake, and lots of fun games!"

I made sure everyone had the address to the park. Only Sally was coming in Dad's car with me, while the rest of my classmates had to find the way to the park themselves.

Dad came to pick me up. Eunice was riding in the shotgun seat. Eunice is my babysitter, and she's the one who usually picks me up from school. But not today. Dad had said he'd leave work early so he could set up for the party.

"Are you ready for the party, Mindy?" Dad asked with a big smile on his face.

"More than ready!"

Sally and I got into the back seat. I couldn't keep

still for the entire car ride. I was too excited for the party and the possibility of getting the puppy!

"I hope you like the decorations, Mindy," Dad said. "Julie and I have been hard at work since noon."

"Wow, Julie left work early to help out too?"

"Yup," Dad said. "She said she wanted to be there for your special day!"

Julie was my dad's new girlfriend. They'd just started officially dating a few weeks ago, but she was really nice and made Dad happy, so I liked her already!

On our way to the park, Sally whispered in my ear, "Hey, so do you really think you're getting a puppy today?"

"I hope so!" I whispered back. "It's all I want this year."

"I hope you get one too!" Sally replied. "What kind of dog do you want?"

I shrugged. I had favorite dog breeds, but when it came to actually getting a dog, I only cared about one thing.

"Whatever dog needs a good home!" I replied. "I've been looking at the dogs in the shelter for several months now, and every dog looks so cute but also really sad."

"Aw, yeah, shelter dogs always look so sad."

Just then I looked up, in time to see Dad glancing up at me in the rearview mirror! When our eyes met, though, he quickly glanced back to the road.

Could he hear Sally and me? Did this mean that he'd gotten me a puppy?

I had so many questions, and even though my heart was beating really fast, I didn't say anything. Hopefully, this would all be worth it in the end!

Chapter 3

When we got to the park, my jaw dropped open when I saw the picnic area. The trees around the picnic tables were decorated with pink and white balloons, while the tables themselves were covered with sky-blue tablecloths. Plates of yummy Korean food, pizza, and board games that everyone could play filled the tables. And that wasn't all! On one of the tables there was a huge mint chocolate chip ice cream cake with the words HAPPY BIRTHDAY, MINDY! written in pink frosting.

Julie and Mrs. Park, Eunice's mom, were finishing setting up. They gave us a wave when they saw Dad's car pull up to the parking space.

"Appa! Everything is so perfect!"

I gave Dad a big hug after we got out of the car. "Thank you so much!"

"You're welcome, Mindy," Dad said. "But I couldn't have done it alone, so be sure to thank Julie and Mrs. Park."

"Thank you so much!" I yelled with my hands cupped together.

Everyone laughed.

"I meant you should thank them when we're closer, but that works too," Dad said with a smile.

Sally and I jumped in to help prepare for the party before the guests arrived. We only had thirty minutes until people were supposed to start showing up! That seemed like a lot of time, but it wasn't when I thought about how much work we had to do.

As I was helping, I sneakily looked around for anything that could be a puppy. But the only presents on the table were much too small to be a puppy, unless Dad had gotten me a teacup Chihuahua.

I tried really hard not to be sad. Maybe I was wrong about a puppy after all.

Soon, though, the guests arrived, and I forgot about the puppy. We played lots of fun games, both Korean and American. We also played a big game of hide-and-seek in the playground and in the park! It was so fun!

When my party was almost over, Dad gathered everyone at the table with the cake.

"All right, everyone," he said. "It's time for cake and presents."

Everyone sang "Happy Birthday" to me, like they did in class. Only this time, some people got really into it. Dad sang into a spoon like he was singing karaoke! He was pretty off-key and made the people next to him wince, but it made me laugh. Dad was so funny.

Soon it was time for me to blow the candles out. It was official. I was really eight!

After that, I opened my presents. Everyone knew I liked dogs, so I got lots of new stuffed dogs and dog T-shirts. People also knew that I loved food, so they got me gift cards that I could spend on yummy things!

Although I was happy with my presents, with every box I opened, the more sure I became that I wasn't going to get a dog today. I was disappointed, but it was okay. Today was a perfect birthday, even without a puppy!

That's when I realized that Dad was nowhere to be found. I got really excited, and my hands started shaking so much that Sally had to help me open the next present. Could this mean what I thought it did?

Just then, Sally pointed and said, "Mindy, look over there!"

Everyone looked up and cheered.

Dad was coming our way with a really cute puppy. I wasn't sure what breed it was, but it didn't matter. To me, it was perfect. It had a big sky-blue bow on the back of its collar.

"Appa!" I squealed. "Is that *my* puppy?"

At the sound of my voice, the dog perked its ears and started running. I scooped it up and gave it a big hug, and it licked my face. I was so happy that I was crying.

People went "aww" as I gave Dad a big hug with the puppy smooshed in between us.

"Mindy, I know you've been wanting a dog for the longest time, and it is a lot of responsibility. But I think you're now ready."

"Don't worry, Dad," I said. "I promise to take good care of it and train it really well!"

"Plus, you can always ask me for help!" Eunice chimed in.

"And me!" Sally said. "You know we have two dogs at home."

"Thank you so much!" I replied to everyone.

I was so happy. This really was the perfect birthday!

Chapter 4

After everyone left and we finished cleaning up at the park, Dad and I went back home with my new four-legged friend. I checked to see if it was a boy or a girl. It was a boy puppy!

The shelter that Dad had adopted him from had given us a crate, and he was now in the crate to keep him safe during the drive. I held the crate tightly so it wouldn't slide around much. It could have just been my imagination, but he kind of looked grateful.

"Do you know what you're going to name him?" Dad asked.

I looked into the crate, where the puppy was

staring back at me with large, round eyes. He was trembling a little, like he was scared, but he still had a cute smile on his bushy face.

"Theodore!" I loudly declared. "Theodore the Mutt."

Dad laughed. "That's a peculiar name for a dog, Mindy."

I shrugged. "He just looks like a Theodore." It was because his bushy face kind of reminded of Teddy Roosevelt's mustache. We'd just learned about Theodore Roosevelt in class this week!

I didn't tell Dad, though. He'd probably think it was weird.

I was really excited to let Theodore out when we got home. He looked so lonely and sad in his crate!

"Are we close to home yet?" I asked Dad.

"We're five minutes away, Mindy," he replied. "Almost there."

"Okay."

I stuck my fingers into the crate so Theodore

would know I was right next to him. He licked my fingers! His tongue felt soft and wet. It tickled!

I giggled. "You're so sweet!"

Dad looked at me through the rearview mirror and smiled. "I'm so glad you two are getting along already!"

At home, Dad set Theodore's crate down on the floor and opened the door.

Theodore immediately dashed out of the crate, barking loudly as his paws clattered all over the floor.

"Whoa!" Dad exclaimed.

"Here, Theodore!" I said. "Come here, buddy!"

But Theodore just kept running around and barking. He jumped on the couch and knocked over Dad's favorite cushions, then dashed up the stairs, only to run down them again.

"Jeez, I hope he calms down," Dad said. "Maybe we can distract him with some of the treats I bought from the pet store."

"That's a great idea, Dad!"

Dad went back out to the car to grab the bag of treats from his car. Alone in the house, I tried my best to get Theodore's attention.

"Theodore! Hey, buddy! Calm down!"

But it was no use. The dog just kept running. He got a hold of the blanket on the couch and started pulling on it.

I took the other end of the blanket and started pulling it, too. Theodore wagged his tail, like he thought it was a game.

"No!" I said. "Bad dog!"

I tried to wrestle the blanket away from him, but it was no use. And then the worst thing happened. The blanket tore!

At that moment, Dad came back with the bag of treats.

"Oh no!" He exclaimed. "That blanket was your mom's!"

He looked really sad, and I felt terrible. I was also really afraid, because this was Theodore's first day at home and he'd already caused trouble. The way Dad was looking at Theodore was not good. He looked kind of mad!

"Theodore, come here!" Dad said in a very firm voice. It was the voice he used when I was in big trouble.

Dad opened the bag of treats, and it was like magic. Theodore let go of the torn blanket right in front of Dad and stared up at him while panting with his tongue out.

I took a treat from the bag and waved it in front of Theodore.

"Sit!"

The puppy didn't do anything.

"Hmm," Dad said. "I guess he isn't trained yet. Are you up for training him, Mindy?"

He was still looking at the torn blanket, and I got really nervous. What if Theodore continued to be bad, and Dad returned him to the shelter?

I tightly squeezed my fists. I couldn't let that happen, no matter what.

"I sure am!" I said really loudly. I was determined to make Theodore the best behaved and best trained dog ever. That way, Dad wouldn't even *think* about returning poor Theodore to the shelter!

After trying to make him sit a few more times, I gave Theodore the treat anyway. At least he wasn't running around the house anymore!

By then it was bedtime, and since Theodore wasn't potty trained yet, Dad had to put him back inside his crate.

"I'll see you in the morning, Theodore," I whispered, putting my face up against the door of the crate. "Good night!"

As soon as Dad and I went up the stairs, Theodore started whimpering.

"We're just going to have to ignore him for now, Mindy," Dad said. "He can sleep with you on your bed after he's house-trained!"

After Dad had tucked me in and gone back downstairs, I tried to ignore Theodore's cries like Dad said I should. But his voice was really loud, and he sounded so sad!

I wanted to cry.

It's okay, Theodore! I thought. *Soon I'll teach*

you how to be a good dog so you can come sleep in my room!

Tomorrow was a Saturday, which meant I could spend a lot of time with Theodore. I was determined to make him the best-behaved dog ever!

Chapter 5

The next day, Eunice came over to help me potty train Theodore.

"Okay," she said. "So, the first thing you need to know about puppies is that they have very small bladders. That means they have to go potty all the time. Since you're at school and your dad has to go to work, you should probably put Theodore in the bathroom with puppy pads so he can go when no one's home. And you have to train him so he knows he should go on the pads. I'll show you how!"

Eunice and I went over to where Theodore already was, in the bathroom. We were keeping him in a pen in the bathroom for now, since it was too mean to have him locked up in the crate all day, and Dad said he didn't want him to roam around the house until he was trained. I think he was scared Theodore might make a mess like last night.

Theodore stood at the edge of the pen and stared at us with his large eyes as he wagged his tail.

We just stared back at him. When we didn't do anything for a while, he whined and whimpered.

"So, we just watch him until he goes?" I guessed. "And then give him a treat?"

"Well, just for the first time, yeah. You can go do something else for a few hours after that . . . probably two or three. Until he needs to go again. Then try to get him to go on the pads, and if he does, give him another treat!"

While we were waiting for Theodore to pee, Eunice and I watched a Korean drama on her phone. Korean dramas are Korean TV shows. My mom and I used to watch them together all the time, but I hadn't watched any since she died.

The one Eunice picked was about a girl who

falls in love with an alien. It was kind of weird, but it was funny, too!

Soon enough, Theodore had to pee, and he peed on one of the pads!

"Good boy!" I cheered, and gave him a treat. He looked so happy while he ate!

"And that's it!" Eunice said. "Keep doing this and he'll probably be house-trained within two weeks. Don't get mad at him if he doesn't pee on the pad, though. Because then he'll sneak around the house and keep having accidents."

"Okay!" I said. It seemed easy enough!

After Eunice left, Dad let me use his tablet so I could look up how to train Theodore to do other things. That seemed pretty straightforward too! All I had to do was give Theodore a treat whenever he did what I told him to do.

I was so excited! I was going to train Theodore to do all kinds of cool stuff, like dance and play dead! It was going to be easy-peasy.

After dinner, I went back into the bathroom to hang out with Theodore.

I held out a treat in front of me as I pointed at the floor.

"Theodore, sit!"

Theodore just stared back at me.

"Sit, boy! Sit, Theodore!"

I tried a couple more times, but it was no use. I thought long and hard about what to do. And then I got an idea.

I approached Theodore, and this time I slowly moved my hand above his head so he had to back away from me. "Theodore, sit!"

It worked! As he backed away, Theodore sat down to make space for me.

"Good boy!"

Like Eunice said I should do, I gave Theodore the treat. He happily munched on it before standing up again.

I tried making him sit again. This time, it only took two more tries before Theodore sat down.

"Good boy! You're so smart!"

That night, I said good-bye to Theodore before I went to bed again.

"You're doing so great, buddy!" I said. "Soon you'll be completely trained and an expert in dog manners. And then you can go wherever you want in the house."

Theodore whined and whimpered again throughout the night, and I hugged Mr. Shiba, my Shiba Inu stuffed doll, tight.

I couldn't wait for the day I could sleep in my bed with my real dog!

Chapter 6

After teaching Theodore some more training basics, Dad and I decided to take him to a dog park. He was starting to look lonely all by himself at home.

The dog park was in a fenced area with lots of trees. There were a ton of dogs already playing in the park, including a golden retriever, a corgi, a husky, and a Westie! All the big dogs were on one side of the park, while the small dogs were on the other. They were separated by a big fence.

"It's so the big dogs don't hurt the little dogs," Dad explained when I asked him about the fence.

All the dogs were so cute! I couldn't wait to say

hi to everyone! And I couldn't wait for Theodore to become friends with them.

"Look, Theodore!" I said. "So many friends!"

I glanced down at him, expecting him to be wagging his tail. Instead Theodore was hiding behind me with his tail tucked between his hind legs.

"Aw, what's wrong, buddy?"

I knelt down so I was face to face with Theodore. He was shaking. He looked really scared!

"Hey," I said softly, patting him on the head. "It's okay. I'm sure the dogs are really nice! You'll go on the side with the small dogs, so it'll be okay! Dad and I will keep you safe, I promise!"

But Theodore still looked scared. When I tried to lead him toward the dog park, he tugged the opposite way on his leash.

Suddenly I wasn't so sure if this was a good idea. Theodore's ears drooped a little, and the sad look in his eyes reminded me of how scared I was on the first day at my new school.

"Being the new kid is always hard, but you can

do it!" I said. "I believe in you! Let's go make new friends!"

I started running toward the park, and Theodore followed me.

"Wait, Mindy!" Dad said. "Slow down or you'll get the other dogs too riled up."

I looked up to see that Dad was right. The dogs that'd been playing near the gate stopped to stare at us. A few of the mean-looking ones started to bark!

More slowly this time, Dad and I led Theodore to the gate of the dog park. As soon as we went inside, the Westie came over, wagging its tail.

"Look, Theodore, a new friend! Be sure to play nice!"

But before Theodore could sniff the other dog, another dog—a Maltese—started yapping and snapping at him!

Theodore yelped and ran back to hide behind me.

I waved at the barking Maltese.

"Go away, you little pipsqueak! Leave Theodore alone!"

"Sorry!" said a fancy-looking lady as she came running over to us. "No, Priscilla!" she said to the Maltese. "Bad girl!"

She scooped the tiny dog into her arms and walked away from us.

The Westie came closer again, sniffing around Theodore. But this time Theodore shrank back and froze until the dog left.

Dad sighed. "Mindy, I don't think Theodore is ready to make friends yet. It doesn't seem like he's good with other dogs."

"He's just shy!" I said. "He only needs a bit of encouragement!"

It made me really sad that Theodore was having so much trouble making friends. If only he weren't so afraid of other dogs!

I gently reached behind me and gave Theodore a little shove. "Go play, boy!"

After a few more shoves, Theodore went off running and made a few laps of the park. The other dogs started chasing Theodore.

"That's it! Play!"

But then a shih tzu snapped at him, and Theodore yelped.

"Theodore, no!"

The other dogs ran away when I bolted toward them. "Leave him alone!"

When I scooped him into my arms, Theodore was shaking so much. I felt really bad for pushing him.

A very tall man came toward us.

"Hey, sorry, guys," he said. "But honestly, your dog doesn't look like he's having any fun. You should take him back home."

I expected Dad to tell the man he was being really rude. But instead Dad didn't say anything. He frowned as the man walked away and then said again, "I don't think he's ready, Mindy. We should leave before something bad happens."

The other dogs were watching Theodore now. Their owners looked really wary too. I was so sad. Why couldn't everyone be nicer to Theodore? He was the new kid!

I put the leash back on Theodore and led him out of the fenced area.

"It's okay, Theodore," I said. "We can try again another day."

Chapter 7

Back home, Dad and I decided Theodore needed a bath. It was going to be his first one! I did my research, and the Internet said we should fill the tub so it went halfway up Theodore's legs and make sure that Theodore didn't get water in his ears.

My bathtub was too small for the three of us, so Dad and I took Theodore to the master bathroom. Dad got in the bath first and made sure the water wasn't too hot for Theodore or me.

"Okay, I think it's ready!" he said after a few minutes.

I picked up Theodore and carefully got into the bath with him. Dad and I were both wearing shorts, so the water didn't make our clothes wet.

Gently, I lowered Theodore into the water. The moment he touched the water, his ears flattened against his head and he whimpered.

"I guess he doesn't like water," Dad said. "That's too bad. I heard some dogs like to swim."

The thought of Theodore swimming made me giggle. He was so small that it was hard to imagine him bravely moving in the water. Maybe he could when he was more grown-up!

Theodore was trembling from head to toe. He looked really scared.

"It's okay, buddy," I said. "It's just water!"

Gently, I scooped a handful of the lukewarm water and lightly splashed it on him. He sniffed my still-wet hand and licked it. It tickled!

Dad and I carefully splashed water on Theodore until his entire body was wet. Damp, Theodore looked really funny, and he was a lot skinnier, too! He looked more like a big mouse than a dog.

Dad put some oatmeal-scented dog shampoo onto his hands and scrubbed it into Theodore's fur.

Theodore stood still, and even closed his eyes a little bit.

I giggled. "He's liking your massage, Dad!"

Dad smiled. It was the first time I'd seen him smile because of Theodore!

I reached out and helped spread the shampoo all over Theodore. He was still shaking, but luckily, he was keeping still. He was being such a good boy!

"Good boy, Theodore!" I said. "I'll give you a brand-new bone after this. You totally deserve one!"

He wagged his tail, like he knew what I was saying. Dad and I grinned at each other.

Even though taking care of him was a lot of work, Theodore was so cute that it was all worth it. And I was really glad I had Dad by my side to help me!

Chapter 8

Monday I had to go back to school. Saying good-bye to Theodore was so hard! I gave him a big hug before Dad and I left the house.

"He'll be fine, Mindy. Don't worry," said Dad. "You'll be back home before you know it."

When I started closing the bathroom door, Theodore lay down on the floor and stared up at me with sad eyes.

"I'll be back soon, buddy," I said. "I promise!"

The school day seemed really long, a thousand billion times longer than usual. I kept staring at the clock on the classroom wall.

During lunch, everyone who was at my birthday party asked me about my puppy.

"What did you name him?" Dill wanted to know.

"Theodore!"

"Theodore?" Dill asked. "Why did you name him that?"

I shrugged. "He looked like a Theodore! Kind of like Teddy Roosevelt."

Everyone at my table giggled.

"Well, I think the name is perfect and cute," Sally said. I could always count on her to have my back! "How is potty training going?"

I told my friends all about my weekend with Theodore.

"You should give him peanut butter when he's a good boy!" said Dill. "Dogs love peanut butter!"

"But don't give him chocolate. It's poisonous."

"Get a bell chain and hang it on the doorknob so he can ring the bell whenever he needs to go potty outside!"

Everyone had such good tips! But then some

people had really silly suggestions like:

"Throw him in the water and it'll teach him how to swim!"

"Wear a mask and run around while chasing him!"

The boys who suggested this laughed and high-fived each other.

Sally rolled her eyes. "Ugh," she said. "Don't listen to them. They're just being silly."

My friends who couldn't make it to my party said they wanted to see what Theodore looked like. I promised I would bring pictures for our next "What's New with You?" show-and-tell!

After school, Eunice picked me up and drove me back to my house. I was bouncing up and down in my seat during the entire car ride.

Eunice laughed. "I was like that when we first got Oliver, too! The first day away is always hard."

Oliver the Maltese is Eunice's dog. He and I are buddies, even though he only pays attention to me when I have food.

When we arrived, Theodore was so glad to see me that he peed on the floor!

"Gross!" Eunice exclaimed. "It's okay. A lot of puppies do that. Hopefully, he'll grow out of it."

After we cleaned up the mess, we got Theodore's leash so we could take him out for a walk. Eunice told me to pack some treats before we left.

"What do we need those for?" I asked.

Eunice smiled. "You'll see."

Theodore wasn't good at walking with a leash yet. His little legs moved so fast that they became a blur. He tugged and tugged until he coughed because the collar was choking him.

"No, boy, slow down! You're choking yourself!" I said. "Slow down!"

"Here, let me," said Eunice. "The trick is to stop whenever he pulls and only keep going when he calms down. It takes a lot of patience, but he'll get it eventually!"

When Eunice started walking, Theodore wiggled and strained against his leash. Eunice stopped and stood still until he gave up. Only when he was completely still did she start walking again, all the while showing him the treat.

"Okay, now you try," Eunice said, handing me the leash.

"Okay!"

Like Eunice did, I started walking but stopped when he pulled again. It was a really slow process, but I was determined to train Theodore so he could walk with a leash!

We did one loop around the neighborhood park before heading back home.

As we walked, I told Eunice about Theodore's rough day at the dog park. When I was done telling her everything, she said, "I have an idea! How about we introduce him to Oliver? He's pretty nice to other dogs. I think it's because he's a bit older."

"That'd be so great!" I said.

Theodore had another chance to make a friend!

Chapter 9

The next day, after school, I scooped Theodore into my arms and got into Eunice's car. Theodore was scared of riding in the car, but I gave him a tight hug.

"It's okay, boy. Eunice doesn't live far from us, so it'll be a short ride!"

Theodore licked my face. He was so sweet!

Even before we entered Eunice's house, Oliver started barking. His little yips were so loud that we could hear them from outside.

Theodore started barking too. His voice was a little lower but more babyish.

"They're talking to each other already!" I said. I hoped this meant they would become friends really soon.

We walked up to Eunice's door. When she opened it, Oliver shot out of the house, raced around the yard, and then ran back toward us in a white blur!

Theodore yelped and jumped behind me.

"It's okay, Theodore! Oliver just wants to say hi!"

Oliver reached us, and soon he was chasing Theodore. The two dogs ran in circles around me. They were making me dizzy!

Eunice waited for the right moment and then quickly scooped Oliver into her arms.

"Gotcha!" she said.

The small dog squirmed around.

"Here," she said. "Maybe this will help."

She carried Oliver into the house, and Theodore and I followed after her. Once we were all inside, Eunice sat on the living room floor, still hugging Oliver close to her.

I gave Theodore a gentle shove.

"Okay," she said. "Now Theodore should be able to properly meet Oliver."

"Go say hi!"

Theodore sniffed my hands, then cautiously moved toward Oliver. Oliver stuck his head out in Theodore's direction and started barking again.

Theodore froze, and his tail went between his legs.

"It's okay, buddy!" I said. "Oliver is nice!"

I softly pushed Theodore again. He slowly approached Oliver again, sniffing the floor.

And then, finally, Oliver and Theodore were nose to nose!

I crossed my fingers and toes and held my breath as the two dogs sniffed each other. I really hoped they'd get along! Oliver squirmed around in Eunice's grip, but she held tight.

Theodore started wagging his tail, and so did Oliver. So far, so good.

And then Eunice slowly let go of Oliver. This time Oliver didn't run. And neither did Theodore. The two dogs continued sniffing each other, looking really excited. They even sniffed each other's butts!

Eunice and I laughed.

"It's so funny when dogs do that," Eunice said. "It's the dog way of saying hi. Let's find a ball so they can play with each other!"

Eunice picked up a tennis ball that was in the corner of the room. She handed it to me.

"Try throwing it!"

"Okay!" I turned to the dogs. "Theodore! Oliver!"

I waved the ball in front of me. Both dogs turned to look at me, their eyes wide with attention.

I giggled. They were both so cute!

"Wait!" Eunice took out her phone and snapped a picture of the dogs.

"Good thinking!" I said. I couldn't wait to show the picture to Dad!

I circled my arm around and around, like I'd seen baseball pitchers do on TV.

"Ready . . . set . . . go!"

I threw the ball. The two dogs burst into action, their paws skittering across the wooden floor as they ran after it. Theodore and Oliver were about the same size, but Theodore was much faster. He caught the ball! I was so proud.

Oliver ran after Theodore and chased him across the house. Only this time Theodore didn't look afraid. He was having fun!

"It looks like they're getting along!" Eunice said. "That's a relief."

"Yay!"

Eunice got out one of Oliver's tug-of-war toys. "Let's see if they'll play with this!"

She held the toy in front of Oliver, who immediately grabbed the other end. She then gave her end to Theodore. The two dogs growled and played with each other. It was so cute!

We watched the dogs play together for a little while longer, until we got kind of hungry.

"Hey, want some snacks?" Eunice asked. "My mom bought some shrimp crackers from the Korean market. We can snack on them while we continue watching the Korean drama we watched this weekend!"

"Okay! Sounds fun!"

While the dogs kept playing, Eunice and I curled up on her living room couch with the shrimp crackers and watched the Korean drama. While we were laughing at the show together, I thought about how—even though she's my babysitter—Eunice was the first friend I made here in Florida. And until now, Theodore had had no friends, but now he was friends with Oliver!

I was so grateful that Theodore and I had friends like Oliver and Eunice!

Chapter 10

The next day at school, we had to draw our family portrait during art class. At first I was nervous, because everyone at my table was drawing their mom and their dad. I was afraid Dad and I would look lonely.

"What's wrong, Mindy?" asked Sally when she saw that I wasn't drawing anything.

I looked over at her paper. She'd drawn her big, happy family, with her two older sisters, her mom, and her dad. My family would look so small compared to hers!

I was a little sad. But then I got an idea.

I raised my hand.

"Yes, Mindy?" said Mr. Stephenson, the art teacher.

"Can I include my dog in my family portrait? His name is Theodore, and he's an important part of my family!"

A few people in the class giggled. Mr. Stephenson smiled.

"Well, of course, Mindy! Dogs and other pets are definitely important parts of our families. I encourage everyone to include their pets in their drawings!"

The class cheered. Everyone around me started to add their pets into their drawings. There were lots of cute dogs, but also a bunch of other animals too, like cats, hamsters, bunnies, and turtles. Some people even drew their fish!

I drew Theodore first, and then Dad and me. I decided to draw a picture of us in the bathtub, giving Theodore a bath! Getting all three of us in the bathtub was hard, but I made it work.

For Dad and me, I drew smiley faces. I wasn't sure if a smiley face would look good on a dog, so I made Theodore's tongue stick out.

Mr. Stephenson came over to look at my work.

"A family portrait in the bathtub! How creative!" He laughed. "Everyone is so happy!"

I looked down at my drawing and smiled. We *did* look happy! And we were.

Dad, Theodore, and I were our own happy family!

Chapter 11

When Eunice and I got home from school, Theodore greeted us at the door. He jumped and barked. He was so happy to see me! He jumped so much that he knocked me over to the floor.

"Hmm," said Eunice. "It's nice that he's so friendly, but we really need to teach him to not jump on people like that. How about we teach him a few more tricks after we finish our home-work?"

"Sure!"

I finished my homework as fast as I could. We were doing fractions and decimals. I liked fractions and decimals! They were much better compared to my greatest enemy: long division.

After I was done, Eunice checked my answers for any silly mistakes.

"Looks good!" she said. "I'm all set with my homework too. I'll help you teach Theodore a few tricks before I go!"

The first trick we wanted to teach Theodore was "down." Eunice told me to give Theodore a little piece of a treat whenever he went down on all fours instead of jumping on me.

I held a treat out so Theodore could see it. He got really excited and started jumping up and down, trying to get the treat.

"No," I said. "Down. Down!"

"You have to say it more firmly," Eunice said. "Say it like a scary teacher!"

I tried my best to sound like Dr. Mortimer, our scary principal. "Down!"

I softly brushed Theodore off my legs so he was sitting down on the floor.

"Quick!" said Eunice. "Give him a treat now!"

I gave Theodore the treat. But when I got out a new treat, he jumped again.

"It'll probably take a couple more tries," Eunice said. "It's okay, though. He'll get it eventually!"

Dad came home, and Eunice left. At the dinner table, I was so antsy. I wanted to go back to training Theodore so that Dad could see he was a good dog!

"Hey, Mindy. Julie is going to come over for dinner on Friday. Would that be okay with you?"

"Sure!"

Now that Julie was coming over, I *really* wanted to teach Theodore to do a bunch of tricks. Then we could impress Dad *and* Julie at the same time! It was going to be tough, but I had faith in Theodore and me.

"Dad, can I use your tablet?" I said. "I want to look up the best ways to train Theodore!"

"Sure, but be careful not to feed him too many treats, Mindy," said Dad. "We don't want him to be overfed and get a stomachache."

"I won't. I promise!"

There were lots of videos on YouTube on how to train a dog. It was pretty confusing, but I decided to give it a shot!

At first Theodore was really confused too. When I held a treat above him, he jumped and bit my hand!

"Ow!" I said. "No! Bad dog."

Theodore flattened his ears and looked really sorry.

I petted him. "It's okay. I know you didn't mean to hurt me."

Theodore and I went over "down" a few more times. It took him fifteen tries, but at the end he went down when I told him to!

"Good boy!" I said. I was so proud of him! It took him a while, but he got it in the end.

I wanted to teach Theodore a few more tricks, but I was tired. I'd had enough of dog training for today.

At that moment, Dad popped his head into the living room.

"It's time for bed, Mindy," he said.

"Okay," I said.

I looked down at Theodore, who was looking at me with expectant eyes.

"We'll just have to try again tomorrow, Theodore," I said. "I'll teach you how to shake hands and all sorts of other cool stuff by Friday!"

Theodore wagged his tail.

The truth was, after today, I wasn't sure Theodore could learn all those things in time. But as Dad liked to say, "Hope for the best and it'll all work out."

I told Theodore this, and he wagged his tail again.

Chapter 12

The next day, I finished my homework fast so I could have lots of time to train Theodore.

Training Theodore was harder than I thought it would be, but it was still worth it. He tried so hard, and even though it sometimes took him a lot of times to get something right, I loved him so much for trying his best.

On Friday, Dad came home early to prepare dinner. We were making bulgogi and bibimbap! Bulgogi is a yummy Korean barbecue beef dish, while bibimbap is rice mixed with egg, vegetables, and gochujang, a spicy pepper paste.

The bibimbap was easy because all Dad had to

67

do was mix in the sliced vegetables from the Korean market with the spicy pepper paste, eggs, and rice. And Dad had already marinated the meat for the bulgogi, so he just had to cook it.

While Dad heated up the meat on the stove, I helped by putting all the ingredients of the bibimbap into three separate bowls. And Theodore? Well, Theodore couldn't really help, but he walked around following everybody!

He sniffed the air and looked really happy.

"Can we give Theodore some of the meat?" I asked Dad.

"I don't think we should," he replied. "Marinated meat is really bad for dogs."

I couldn't meet Theodore's eyes after that. I felt so bad that he couldn't have any of the meat!

After the meat was done cooking, Dad fried the eggs on the stove and placed them on the bibimbap with some sesame seeds and sesame oil as a finishing touch.

Then we put the bowls of bibimbap and the plate of bulgogi on the dining room table and gave each other a high five. Dad and I were master chefs!

When Julie came, she sniffed the air appreciatively.

"Wow! The food smells so good!" she exclaimed. "I didn't know you were such a good cook, Brian!"

Dad blushed. "I couldn't have done it without Mindy. She helped a lot."

"I sure did!" I said. "But Dad is getting better every day. When we first moved here, he couldn't even reheat dumplings without hurting himself!"

Julie laughed.

Dad looked embarrassed, but he still said, "Aw, thank you, Mindy."

Dinner was so tasty that everyone was in a good mood. Theodore rested his head on my knees while I ate. I wanted to sneak him some food so bad! But I didn't want to hurt him, so I didn't. I hoped he wouldn't hate me for it.

When we were done eating, Dad said, "Mindy and Theodore have something to show us. Right, Mindy?"

I nodded as I got out of my seat and tried not to

look nervous. "Yup! Come here, Theodore!"

Theodore got up, his ears perked and head cocked to the side with attention.

I got some dog treats and went to the living room with Theodore. Dad and Julie sat on the couch to give us their undivided attention.

"First," I said, "the easy-peasy part."

I held a treat in front of me and touched my shoulder with the other hand. "Theodore, sit!"

Theodore blinked up at me, wagging his tail slightly. He sat down.

Dad and Julie clapped.

"Woo-hoo! Go, Theodore!" I cheered.

Theodore's tail went faster, like he knew they were cheering for him. I gave him a treat.

"Okay. Next: Theodore, down."

I pointed at the floor.

Theodore got down flat against the floor.

"Good boy!" I gave him another treat.

"Wow, what a smart dog!" Julie said.

I grinned. "We're only halfway there!"

I turned back to Theodore, who'd gotten back up on his feet. "Okay, Theodore."

I rested a hand in front of him. "Paw!"

Theodore stared at my hand and then at the treat. I held my breath.

Come on boy, I thought. *You can do it!*

He put his paw on my hand.

"Outstanding!" hooted Dad.

"Last but not least . . ." After Theodore had gotten back up on his feet, I bounced the treat up and down above his head. "Dance!"

But instead of dancing, Theodore jumped up.

"No, boy," I said. "Not jump. Dance!"

I tried again.

This time Theodore stared up at my hand. He looked really confused.

"It's okay, Mindy," Dad said. "Maybe that trick is too hard for Theodore."

I shook my head. "No, he can do it. Watch!"

I tried for a third time.

Theodore got up on his hind legs and bounced

up and down like he was supposed to!

Dad and Julie got to their feet and clapped while they cheered. It was a standing ovation!

"Amazing!" said Dad.

"What a good boy!" said Julie.

I gave Theodore a treat and then hugged him. I was so proud of him! It wasn't easy, but we did it!

Chapter 13

That night, Dad tucked Theodore and me into bed. Theodore was pretty good with potty training now, so Dad said he could finally sleep with me in my room!

"You did such a wonderful job training Theodore, Mindy," said Dad. "You've just turned eight, but you're so much more responsible already!"

"I wanted to prove to you that Theodore was a good dog!" I said. "The Internet says that all dogs can be trained, even rescues! People just don't give them a chance."

Dad nodded. "You are so right, Mindy. I see that now. I'm sorry I doubted you and Theodore."

74

He reached over to give Theodore a pat on the head.

Just then, I remembered my drawing. Mr. Stephenson had given me a gold star for it, but I'd forgotten to take it out of my backpack until now.

"Appa, I want to show you something."

"Oh? What is it, Mindy?"

I got up from my bed and gently pulled my drawing from my backpack. It was a little wrinkly, but that was okay.

"We had to draw a family portrait for art class," I said. "And this is what I drew!"

Dad's eyes went wide as he looked at his portrait. "We look so happy!"

"That's what Mr. Stephenson said too! And I agree."

Dad carefully took the drawing from me like it was the most expensive drawing in the entire world. He held it in front of his face and stared even more closely at it. "I'm going to frame this and hang it up. This is a really nice drawing, Mindy. Thank you for sharing it with me."

I beamed with pride. "You're welcome!"

"The three of us really are a happy family, aren't we?" Dad said, sounding thoughtful. His eyes looked a little shiny as he smiled.

"Yup!"

"I'm so grateful for you, Mindy," Dad said. "And you too, Theodore."

He gave Theodore another pat on the head. Theodore wagged his tail.

"I love you, Dad," I said.

"I love you too, Mindy. And . . . yes, you too, Theodore. Now good night, you two."

Dad turned off the lights and left my room, still carefully holding the drawing.

I petted Theodore.

"You hear that, Theodore? Dad said he loves you. And *I* love you even more! You are so loved!"

Theodore licked my hand, and I giggled.

This was the beginning of a beautiful friendship.

Acknowledgments

First and foremost, I'd like to thank my parents, who got me a puppy for my tenth birthday and made my childhood dream come true. This book is largely based on that experience, even though Mindy is only eight when she gets her dog. (Lucky duck!)

I would next like to thank all the teachers, librarians, booksellers, and students I met while I was on tour over the past year. Thank you so much for loving Mindy and for accepting her into your hearts. Mindy is really lucky to have friends like you!

Thank you also to all the parents who bought the Mindy Kim books and/or reached out to me over social media to tell me how much their kids are loving Mindy. Your messages always brighten my world, even on my worst days. Thank you for sharing the Mindy Kim series and other books with your kids to foster their love of reading. You're all rock stars.

Like any book I write, this book wouldn't have been possible without the support of my friends, who remind me to take care of myself and have fun whenever life gets stressful. Thank you for hanging out with me and for making my last couple of months a little bit brighter. I already mentioned most of them in my previous books, but here's a special shout-out to Chelsea Chang, Shiyun Sun, Luke Chou, Bernice Yau, Alice Zhu, Steven Bell, Sherry Yang, Kelly Huang, Kaiti Liu, and Stephanie Liu. A whole other separate mention goes to Aneeqah Naeem, who's once again sitting across the table from me as I write this. I consider myself really fortunate to have friends like you.

Lastly, thank you always to Alyson Heller, Penny Moore, Cassie Malmo, and Jenny Lu. Thank you for all that you do to support Mindy and me. We're so lucky to have a team like you! And of course, thank you to Dung Ho for her always spot-on illustrations that bring Mindy and her adventures to life.

Don't miss Mindy's next adventure!

About the Author

Lyla Lee is the author of the Mindy Kim series as well as the upcoming YA novel *I'll Be the One*. Although she was born in a small town in South Korea, she's since then lived in various parts of the United States, including California, Florida, and Texas. Inspired by her English teacher, she started writing her own stories in fourth grade and finished her first novel at the age of fourteen. After working various jobs in Hollywood and studying psychology and cinematic arts at the University of Southern California, she now lives in Dallas, Texas. When she is not writing, she is teaching kids, petting cute dogs, and searching for the perfect bowl of shaved ice. You can visit her online at lylaleebooks.com.